THE ADVENTURES OF TINY FROG

Authored by
Micah Christopher

Illustrated by
Lynne Hudson

6

CHAPTER 1
The Little Figure

Tiny Frog woke up to the smell of pancakes. He jumped out of bed and scrambled down the hallway to meet his father, Mr. Frog.

"Good morning," said Mr. Frog.

"Good morning," said Tiny Frog.

Tiny Frog looked out the window, his eyes as wide as saucers, and what he saw took his breath away. He jumped for joy. He scrambled to Mr. Frog to tell him the big news. The lake was rising which meant that it was better for Turtle to swim. When Mr. Frog heard the big news he let out a gasp.

Mrs. Frog came downstairs when she heard all of the commotion.

"What is wrong, dear?" she asked Mr. Frog.

Mr. Frog was speechless. Finally he managed to get a few words out. "Turtle asked me to pray over him before he went swimming for the first time! But I don't know where he is. He is usually sunbathing on that log."

Mrs. Frog took a deep breath. "He probably went for a walk this morning, dear. Thank you for doing such a nice labor by praying over him."

Mrs. Frog patted Mr. Frog on the shoulder. "It will be alright, dear."

Mr. Frog was uplifted by Mrs. Frog's words, but he was still worried. Mr. Frog hurried to get his and Tiny Frog's coats.

"Where are you going?" Mrs. Frog asked.

"We're going outside because we need to find Turtle," Mr. Frog answered.

"Wait! You need to eat breakfast. Come back!" Mrs. Frog shouted.

But Mr. Frog and Tiny Frog had already gone out the door and were hurrying down the path.

Mr. Frog bent down sadly and told Tiny Frog, "If we do not find Turtle, we will send a team to search the shoreline."

This gave Tiny Frog chills.

Mr. Frog and Tiny Frog continued on the path. Tiny Frog could hear Mr. Frog mumbling to himself.

Finally Mr. Frog shouted, "Over there—movement!"

A jolt of excitement rushed through Tiny Frog as he heard his father's voice. Mr. Frog took off in a run down the path with Tiny Frog hot on his heels. As they came close to the movement, Mr. Frog said, "It was just some leaves in the wind."

Tiny Frog could see that Mr. Frog was sad. Tiny Frog tried to cheer him up but it didn't work. Then they heard a tiny squeaky shout.

"What was that?" Tiny Frog asked in alarm.

"It was probably just a bird…" Mr. Frog's words trailed off.

All of a sudden Mr. Frog and Tiny Frog saw a small figure running down the muddy path.

Mr. Frog and Tiny Frog were shocked. As the figure came closer, Mr. Frog wondered if they needed to run, but they stood silently.

When the figure was right in front of them, Mr. Frog could see that it was a tiny brown mouse in a brown jacket with a blue scarf. The mouse looked at them with curiosity in his brown eyes.

The mouse was speechless. Then Mr. Frog and Tiny Frog saw seven more small figures running down the path. When the seven figures came up to the first mouse, the elder mice introduced themselves.

"Hi, my name is Finch," said the dad mouse.

Then the second elder mouse introduced herself.

"Hi, my name is Rose," she said in her squeaky voice. "And these are all my children. We have Asher, Piper, Tiny, Whistler, Lila and Max."

"Ahhhh, hi," said Mr. Frog in a croaky voice.

The two mice were astonished. Now it was Tiny Frog's turn to introduce himself.

"Hi, I'm Tiny Frog," he said.

The two elder mice giggled and then said with joy, "Follow us." The mice and their six light brown children turned around and started to scamper down the path.

CHAPTER 2
The Mouse Family

Mr. Frog and Tiny Frog followed the mouse family down the muddy path. After a short walk, Tiny Frog saw a decent sized maple tree with a small hole in-between its roots.

"You are welcome inside, we have pies!" said Finch.

Tiny Frog tried to squeeze inside the little hole in the tree. But he could only stick his arm in.

"Sorry," said Tiny Frog. "I cannot seem to fit in here."

"Ok, that's alright," said Finch.

"I'll go get the pies," said Rose. "We will have a picnic in the meadow."

Rose entered the house and she came out with four small pies. The first one smelled like apple pie. The second smelled like raspberry pie. By now, Tiny Frog's mouth was watering. The third pie smelled like cranberry. The fourth pumpkin.

At the meadow the birds were singing their early songs, and bumble bees were humming their tunes. Rose spread the red checkered picnic cloth out on the grass. She began to take out and unwrap the warm pies, and then cut them into slices.

Tiny Frog thought the pies were delicious, even though they were only tiny morsels for him.

Mr. Frog cleared his throat. "Well we have to get going. Thank you for the scrumptious pies."

The mice gathered around them and said their farewells.

Mr. Frog led the way. Tiny Frog trailed behind him at his heels. Tiny Frog was sad to leave the mice.

CHAPTER 3
Tiny Frog and the Kingfisher

Mr. Frog and Tiny Frog started to go home. There was a clattering chill in the breeze. While they tromped down upon the forest floor path, they saw a strange rock. It was brown. Mr. Frog moved a little closer. Then it started to move. Startled, they jumped back. They turned around and ran down the path, splitting directions.

Tiny Frog hopped with all his might, adrenaline pumping through his legs, until he couldn't. He wondered what that brown rock was. Then he was interrupted from his thoughts by a big shadow casting over the ground. He looked up and it was a big kingfisher. The kingfisher swooped down and skidded to a stop.

The kingfisher looked at him with compassion in his eyes. "Are you lost?" he asked.

"Yes, sir," Tiny Frog replied.

"Well I think I can help you."

"Thank you, sir."

"My pleasure," said the kingfisher. The kingfisher got right to it. He turned to Tiny Frog. "Hop on my back."

Tiny Frog hesitated nervously, but then with all his strength he climbed onto the kingfisher's back.

He grasped onto the kingfisher's blue-gray feathers. The kingfisher jumped onto a rock, and with two mighty flaps, he sprung into the air. Tiny Frog thought it was exhilarating. He felt the soft breeze on his face and watched as the trees whizzed under him. All of a sudden, he saw a vast, deep blue river below, and it glimmered in the morning light.

The kingfisher spoke up. "Where is your house?"

"It is by the creek," explained Tiny Frog.

"A little past the thicket."

The kingfisher flew on. Then Tiny Frog saw his house on a bank off of Blueberry Thicket Lake. He loved to go blueberry picking in the summer.

"Over there!" shouted Tiny Frog.

"Hang on!" said the kingfisher.

The kingfisher took a sharp turn right. Swooping down, the kingfisher landed at Tiny Frog's door. Tiny Frog got off the kingfisher's back.

Tiny Frog looked at him. "Thank you so much! I don't know what I would have done without you."

"May you please look for my dad? He is wearing a brown coat with a green scarf. He should be near Boulder Rock."

The kingfisher bowed in loyalty. "Of course, Tiny Frog. Goodbye."

"Goodbye," said Tiny Frog.

With that, the kingfisher jumped into the air.

"Come back soon!" Tiny Frog called out.

Do not be afraid for
I am with you
Blueberries

Then he went inside. Mrs. Frog was in the kitchen washing the dishes from the morning.

"Hello, Tiny Frog," she said.

"Hello," Tiny Frog panted.

"Where have you been?" Mrs. Frog asked. Tiny Frog was covered with dried mud and leaves.

But Tiny Frog was already in his room getting ready to go camping. He had to ask Mrs. Frog if it was ok first. So he raced down the hallway.

"Mom, can I go camping? Dad and I got split up and I want to go camping near Boulder Rock to find him. I'll only be gone for about two days. I asked a friendly kingfisher if he would look for Dad too. Pleeeease?"

"Why sure! That sounds wonderful! You'll find him soon! We will start packing right away!"

Mrs. Frog led Tiny Frog down the hall and entered his room.

"Where's your backpack?" she asked.

"Over there in my closet," Tiny Frog said.

Mrs. Frog walked over to the closet and started rummaging through bins and drawers. Finally she found it. A brown backpack with several pouches on the front. Mrs. Frog looked over at Tiny Frog.

"Where's your box of matches and your pocket knife?" asked Mrs. Frog.

"In my lock box," Tiny Frog replied.

CHAPTER 4
Tiny Frog's Camping Trip

Tiny Frog trudged through the forest, as a soft breeze blew through the canopy of trees. Finally by a little lake he found the perfect camping spot. He got right to it. First, he set up the tent. The tent was blue with a window on each side.

Then he found stones by the lake and built a fire pit. He added kindling and a fire starter. Then he placed pieces of wood on top of the kindling. He took out his box of matches and started a good fire.

After he grabbed his camping chair, he got the package of hot dogs and carefully picked out the hot dogs with the tongs he brought.

Then by the edge of his campsite, he found two good sturdy sticks. He used the sticks to roast the hot dogs on the fire. After a good meal, he sat by the fire gazing into the hot coals. Boulder Rock looked majestic in the setting sun.

After a while, he got tired. So he poured a little water from his canteen onto the fire pit. Then he crawled into his sleeping bag and had a good night's sleep.

In the morning, he woke up to the birds singing and the sun beams breaking through the tops of the trees.

He slipped out of his sleeping bag and crawled out of the tent. He quickly walked over to the pile of wood, and put some kindling in the fire pit with a fire starter. Then he added some heavy pieces of wood.

He got out his box of matches and started another blazing fire. He had a nice morning listening to the birds and watching the fire.

Suddenly, he heard a familiar cry from above. "Tiny Frog," someone said.

Tiny Frog looked up and saw that it was the kingfisher he met yesterday!

The kingfisher swooped down and landed with a soft flutter of his wings. Tiny Frog noticed something on the kingfisher's back.

"Tiny Frog!" cried Mr. Frog.

"Dad?" shouted Tiny Frog.

Mr. Frog slipped off of the kingfisher's back.

Mr. Frog and Tiny Frog embraced.

**Tiny Frog stepped back.
"How did you get here?" he asked.
Then the long story began.**

"I was running and I ran until I couldn't. I ended up beside a big stump. I climbed up and sat on it. I started to think, what happened? I wondered what the brown moving rock was. So I pondered it over. And Tiny Frog, do you know what I think it was? I think it was Turtle, because it didn't quite look like a rock at all. The scutes on its back gave me a clue. But there's one problem. I can't remember where we saw him. Tiny Frog, do you remember?"

Tiny Frog thought it over. Finally he said, "I do not. I'm sorry."

Tiny Frog had an idea. He walked over to the kingfisher. "Wait here," Tiny Frog said to Mr. Frog. "I'll be right back."

Tiny Frog started talking earnestly to the kingfisher. Mr. Frog stood there trying to listen to what Tiny Frog was saying.

Then Tiny Frog turned around and walked over to Mr. Frog.

"Dad," he exclaimed. "I have a plan. Since you have longer legs and hop faster, you go to the left and I'll ride the kingfisher to the right. If you find Turtle, blow your whistle hard. Then if I find Turtle I will blow my whistle so that we can communicate. I'll be praying for you."

Tiny Frog climbed onto the kingfisher's back. With three mighty flaps, the kingfisher was off.

He soared high over the rocky outcrops and pine trees. It felt good to be in the air again! The kingfisher scanned the ground, looking for any movement. Then Tiny Frog saw something.

"Right over there!" shouted Tiny Frog. The kingfisher looked around.

"Over where?" he asked in confusion.

"Right by that big pine tree," said Tiny Frog.

"Oh, yeah," said the kingfisher.

He took a turn and dived for the rock. The sharp dive took Tiny Frog's breath away. The kingfisher leveled out again and Tiny Frog took deep breaths, letting the forest air whoosh through his lungs.

When the kingfisher finally landed, he asked, "Where did you say it was again?"

The kingfisher followed Tiny Frog to where he was standing.

He had his arm around something brown that looked like a rock.

"I think it's Turtle," said Tiny Frog.

Tiny Frog cupped his hands around his mouth and hollered, "Is this Turtle?"

Suddenly the brown rock started to move. And slowly a head popped out.

Once Turtle saw Tiny Frog, his eyes gleamed.

"Tiny Frog," he whispered. "I'm lost." Turtle couldn't hold back the tears any longer, and they rushed out like a waterfall.

"It's ok," said Tiny Frog. "I can help you. How did this happen?"

Then Tiny Frog remembered. "Plug your ears, everyone," he said.

He rummaged through his pocket, grasping his whistle. He carefully lifted it to his mouth and blew it hard.

TWEEEEEEET.

Tiny Frog's ears were ringing by the time it stopped.

"Whoah," cried Turtle and the kingfisher. "That was loud!"

"It's the only way I can communicate with Mr. Frog. Sorry."

"Mr. Frog, where is he?" Turtle shouted.

"We were searching for you," said Tiny Frog. "He went to the left and I went to the right."

"Wow, you were brave to come and find me," said Turtle. Now his tears were drying up.

"So what happened?" asked Tiny Frog.

Then another long story began.

"I woke up and I decided that I would go for a stride. You know, for turtles, it's hard to walk fast. So I decided to take my time. Once I got a little down the path, I noticed that it was getting dark. I checked my watch and it was 7:30pm. I started to turn around but realized that I was lost! So I tried calling for help but no one heard me. I decided to keep on walking the way I came. I walked for what felt like a long time, until finally I couldn't. I was so thirsty and hungry. But finally I found a little puddle and a few dried berries, and that got me through the night. When I woke up, I was disheartened and I decided to pray. And when I opened my eyes, I heard and saw you. And that was my story."

Tiny Frog was happy that he found Turtle and so was the kingfisher.

CHAPTER 5
The Kingfisher's Team

Suddenly the kingfisher had an idea.

"I can't carry Turtle and you at the same time. So I was thinking I could get some of my friends and we could put Turtle up in a hammock and all us kingfishers could grab it and carry Turtle while another kingfisher carries you. Then we can bring Turtle safely to the pond. How does that sound, Turtle?"

"That sounds great," said Turtle. "But there's one problem. I've never been high in the air before."

"It's going to be ok," said the kingfisher. "You can watch Tiny Frog go first."

Now it was Tiny Frog's turn to speak up.

"It's really not that scary," Tiny Frog started. "Remember the verse, 'Do not be afraid for I am with you,' in Isaiah? You can say that over and over again when you're in the air and you can close your eyes as well!"

"Thanks for the encouragement," said Turtle.

"Alright, I'll get going now," said the kingfisher. "Meet us back at the campsite!" yelled Tiny Frog.

The kingfisher took off flying high over the treetops.

Tiny Frog turned to turtle again, "Mr. Frog will be here soon. He heard my whistle."

"Good," said Turtle. "How long have you been looking for me?"

"All morning," replied Tiny Frog.

"That was very loyal of you, dear friend."

"Why thank you," said Tiny Frog. "Are you hungry?"

"Yes," said Turtle. "Very."

"What do you like to eat?" questioned Tiny Frog.

"Berries and clams," said Turtle.

"Okay, that is great!" said Tiny Frog. "I have some at the campsite. Do you want to go there now?"

"Sure," said Turtle gratefully.

"That's great!" said Tiny Frog with enthusiasm. "Ok! Let's go."

All of a sudden, Mr. Frog came running and shouting through the woods. He had finally arrived. After a few slaps on the back and joyful bellows of laughter, they all embraced, happy to be with each other.

Tiny Frog, Mr. Frog and Turtle tromped through the woods until they came to the campsite.

Tiny Frog started rummaging through some bags.

"Here are some ripe raspberries!" Tiny Frog said.

"Thank you!" Turtle gobbled the berries up.

Suddenly they heard the flapping of wings. They looked up. The kingfisher and his three friends were hovering over them. Tiny Frog waved at them gratefully.

The kingfishers set the hammock on the ground and Turtle climbed in.

Tiny Frog and Mr. Frog waved goodbye and so did Turtle.

"Goodbye, friend!" Tiny Frog watched as the kingfishers carried Turtle off into the endless light blue sky.

Tiny Frog packed up his bags with sadness. He remembered the previous day and thought about how exciting and scary it had been all at the same time.

THE END

"A friend
loves at
all times,"

Proverbs 17:17 (NIV)

Lionheart Littles

THIS BOOK HAS BEEN WRITTEN
BY A LIONHEART LITTLE

THE GOSPEL:

Jesus has died
on the cross for
your wrongs,
so His grace
has set you FREE.

www.ingramcontent.com/pod-product-compliance
Lightning Source LLC
Chambersburg PA
CBRC101117300726
48978CB00009B/188